BUGS!

by David T. Greenberg

Illustrated by
Lynn Munsinger

SCHOLASTIC INC.

New York Toronto London Auckland Sydney
Mexico City New Delhi Hong Kong

To Sam, my most beautiful and beloved bug of all
D. T. G.

For Andrea
L. M.

ISBN 0-439-07779-6

Text copyright © 1997 by David T. Greenberg.
Illustrations copyright © 1997 by Lynn Munsinger.
All rights reserved.
Published by Scholastic Inc., 555 Broadway, New York, NY 10012,
by arrangement with Little, Brown and Company Inc.
SCHOLASTIC and associated logos are trademarks and/or registered
trademarks of Scholastic Inc.

12 11 10 9 8 7 6 5 4 3 2 1   9/9 0 1 2 3 4/0

Printed in the U.S.A.   24

First Scholastic printing, March 1999

Beetles,
Bedbugs,
Bottle flies,
Tarantulas the size of pies
With lots and lots and lots of eyes—
Staring at you, BUGS!

A million maggots in a vase,
Lice as thick as mayonnaise,

A horsefly that's so huge it neighs—
Glaring at you, BUGS!

Bugs with pincers, claws, and hair,
Bugs much fiercer than a bear,
Buggies in your underwear—
Tearing at you, BUGS!

Oh, in your clothes they're restin',
In your nose they're nestin',
There isn't any question
They're infestin' your intestine.

Yup, loathe 'em or adore bugs,
There's no way to ignore bugs.
So even if you hate 'em,
Why not investigate 'em?

Now, you may have had a hunch
If you bite bugs, they will crunch.
This is true, but stay alert—
The fat ones sometimes squirt.

Perhaps your intuition
'Bout those spit bugs you've been squishin'
Is they're useless. That ain't true—
They're great to barbecue!

But bugs have far more uses
Than for barbecues or juices.
You can do such nifty tricks
With tsetse flies to ticks. . . .

So grab a garden spider,
Saddle her and ride 'er —
Yipee-i-yay, yipee-i-yo,
Rope her at the rodeo.

Rare beyond compare
Is caterpillar hair.
Take a tweezers, yank it,
Weave yourself a blanket.
(Or know what's even better?
A caterpillar sweater.)

There's a microscopic udder
That you'll find on female fleas;
You can milk them and make budder
Or the most delicious cheese.

Teach your centipede to fetch,
Teach her to play dead,
Teach her to go potty
In your mom and daddy's bed.

A scorpion in a string bikini,
A tick wearing only a hat,
A tuxedo on a teeny-weeny
Itsy-bitsy gnat.

Try millipedes for dental floss,
Feel them scrape away the moss;
Drop one down your sister's pants,
Watch her do the boogie dance.

Incandescent fireflies,
Dragonflies and bees—
String them all together
To light up Christmas trees.

Wrapped in cast from head to toe,
Your brother cannot scratch.
Drop termite larvae down the crack;
He'll love it when they hatch.

The flavor of a cricket
Is so sweet that you can lick it;
It's actually far sweeter
Than the flavor of a skeeter.

A bracelet made of butterflies,
A beetle for a brooch,
An earwig for a nose ring,
In your navel, put a roach.

Use spiderwebs for tissues,
They're perfect trampolines,
Roll them into balls
And they taste like jelly beans.

Strap a giant waterbug
Underneath each toe;
You can use them just like water skis
Or walk on H_2O.

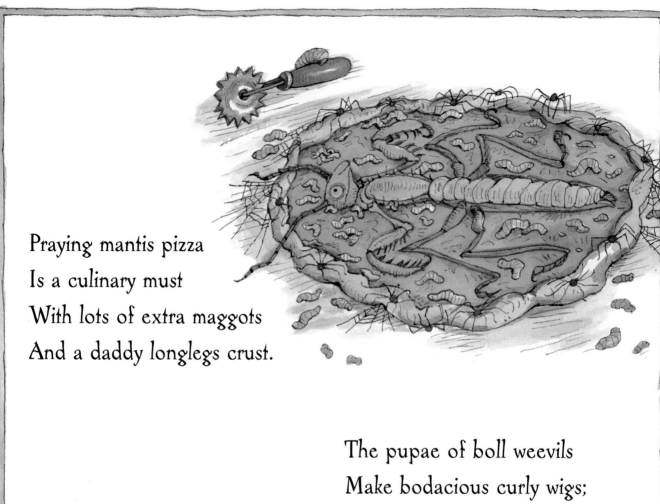

Praying mantis pizza
Is a culinary must
With lots of extra maggots
And a daddy longlegs crust.

The pupae of boll weevils
Make bodacious curly wigs;
For phenomenal fake whiskers,
Love those whirligigs.

Stinkbugs, stinkbugs,
Squish them in your fist,
Drop them in a pepper mill,
Give the crank a twist.

Oh, touching a bug is so yucky to some
That the thought of it makes them sweat,
But bugs are truly fond of us—
They'd like *you* as their pet!

They'll train you to fetch sticks,
To sit, roll over, play dead.

They'll walk you on a leash,
If you're good, they'll scratch your head.

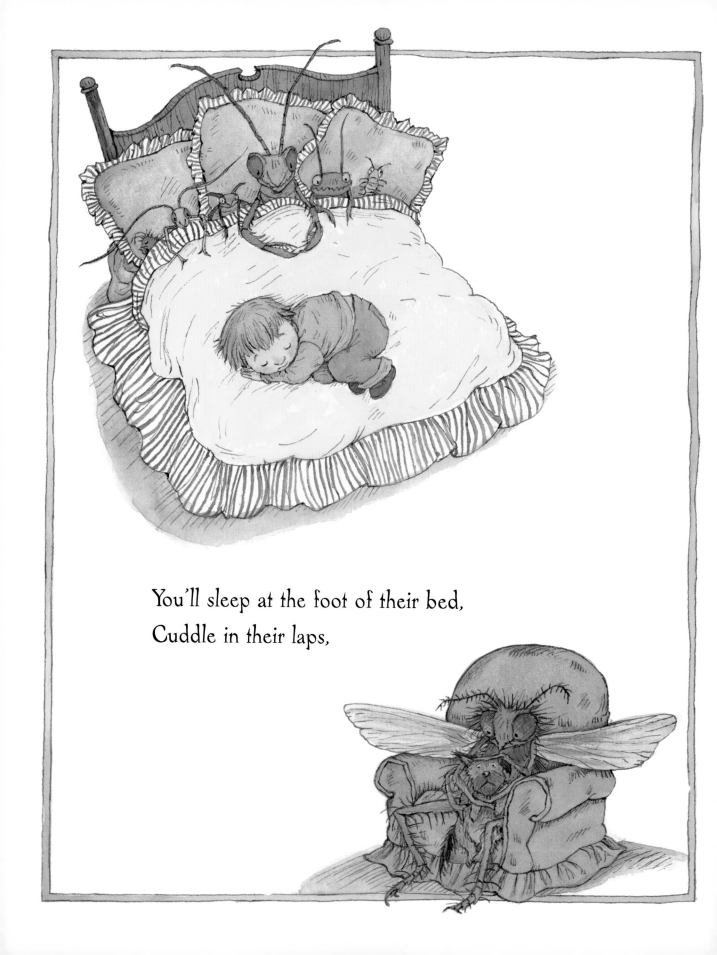

You'll sleep at the foot of their bed,
Cuddle in their laps,

Lick them when you're happy,
Nibble up their scraps.

And then one day they'll polish you
Lovingly with wax,
Attach you to a wall
With bubble gum and tacks.

How lucky can you get?
For that's where you shall stay,
In their *Human Being Collection*
On permanent display.